STAR WARS
WHERE'S THE WOOKIEE?
DELUXE

studio fun
INTERNATIONAL

WANTED

FOR CRIMES AGAINST THE EMPIRE

DEAD
OR ALIVE

REWARD
25,000

CHEWBACCA

This rebel is the number one prize. Despite his towering height and distinctive smell, he is an expert at evading capture.

HAN SOLO

Not to be overshadowed by his mammoth copilot, this charming smuggler is well-known for his criminal activity. Where there's a Chewie, Han won't be far away.

MILLENNIUM FALCON

Home to Han and Chewie, this famous freighter is lightning-fast and rarely at port. If it's not in hyperspace, you might be able to spot it.

GREEDO

Short-tempered and overconfident, this unlucky Rodian was never the most skilled bounty hunter. Chewie shouldn't have too much trouble avoiding this guy.

BOBA FETT

The most notorious bounty hunter in the universe is on Chewie's trail. Beating him to the bounty will not be easy.

THE HUNT IS ON!

Find these characters in every location

DENGAR

This Corellian is held in high regard for his excellent track record of hunting down his mark. Look out for his turban and plated armor.

BOSSK

A fierce warrior and hunter, Bossk is renowned and feared for his success in the Clone Wars. He carries a large mortar gun that fires high impact bolts.

ZUCKUSS

This insectoid is from the planet Gand. You wouldn't want to come face to face with this skilled bounty hunter.

4-LOM

Often employed by the Galactic Empire, this former protocol droid is an expert in hunting down rebel activity.

IG-88

This bounty hunter was once an IG-series assassin droid. Watch out for those sensors, because this droid is fierce competition.

LOCATIONS

Hunt Chewie throughout the galaxy!

Chewie has a sizeable bounty on his head. Rarely seen without his partner-in-crime, Han Solo, this Wookiee has evaded capture on multiple occasions. They make their escape on the fastest freighter in the galaxy, the *Millennium Falcon*.

Can you find this furry criminal before other accomplished bounty hunters beat you to it? These are the locations where Chewie has been known to hide.

JAWA MARKET

HOTH

GEONOSIS

CORUSCANT

MOS EISLEY

STAR DESTROYER

CLOUD CITY

ECHO BASE

THE CANTINA

EWOK VILLAGE

JEDI TEMPLE

THE DEATH STAR

JABBA'S PALACE

IMPERIAL HANGAR

KASHYYYK

JAWA MARKET
The Jawas are in town with some droids to sell. Residents of Tatooine and beyond gather to grab themselves a bargain from these scavengers. Rebels know this is the place to find parts to repair their mechanical companions.

HOTH
Many a battle has been fought between the rebels and Imperials in this dramatic snowscape. The two sides bring their greatest firepower and soldiers to defend their cause, but they have to watch out for Hoth's local predators!

GEONOSIS
In the Outer Rim, on the desert planet of Geonosis, there lives a winged, insectoid species. Geonosians enjoy gladiatorial-style entertainment, with great beasts fighting it out in the famous arena.

CORUSCANT
This bustling Imperial city is seen as the center of Galactic culture. As the home of the Imperial government and the Emperor himself, it's the last place you'd expect to find enemies of the Empire...

MOS EISLEY

A busy day in the marketplace draws visitors from all over the universe. Described once as a "hive of scum and villainy," Mos Eisley plays host to smugglers, black-market traders, and all-around criminal activity—the perfect hiding place for rebels.

STAR DESTROYER
This heavily-armed warship sails through the stars pursuing the rebels. Aboard are the most terrifying commanders in the Imperial fleet, plus a few unlikely visitors.

CLOUD CITY
In the sky above the planet Bespin there is a mining colony surrounded by clouds. Relatively unimportant to the Empire's plans, the city allows rebels to blend in and stay hidden. Or so the rebels think.

ECHO BASE

On the unforgiving plains of Hoth the rebels have found a refuge from the Empire. The base is protected by a deflector shield, and an ion cannon deters any unwanted visitors.

THE CANTINA

This fine establishment is a great place for spacers to enjoy a beverage, listen to music, and engage in a fistfight. It is an ideal spot for outlaws to pick up work, but it can also attract the attention of master bounty hunters.

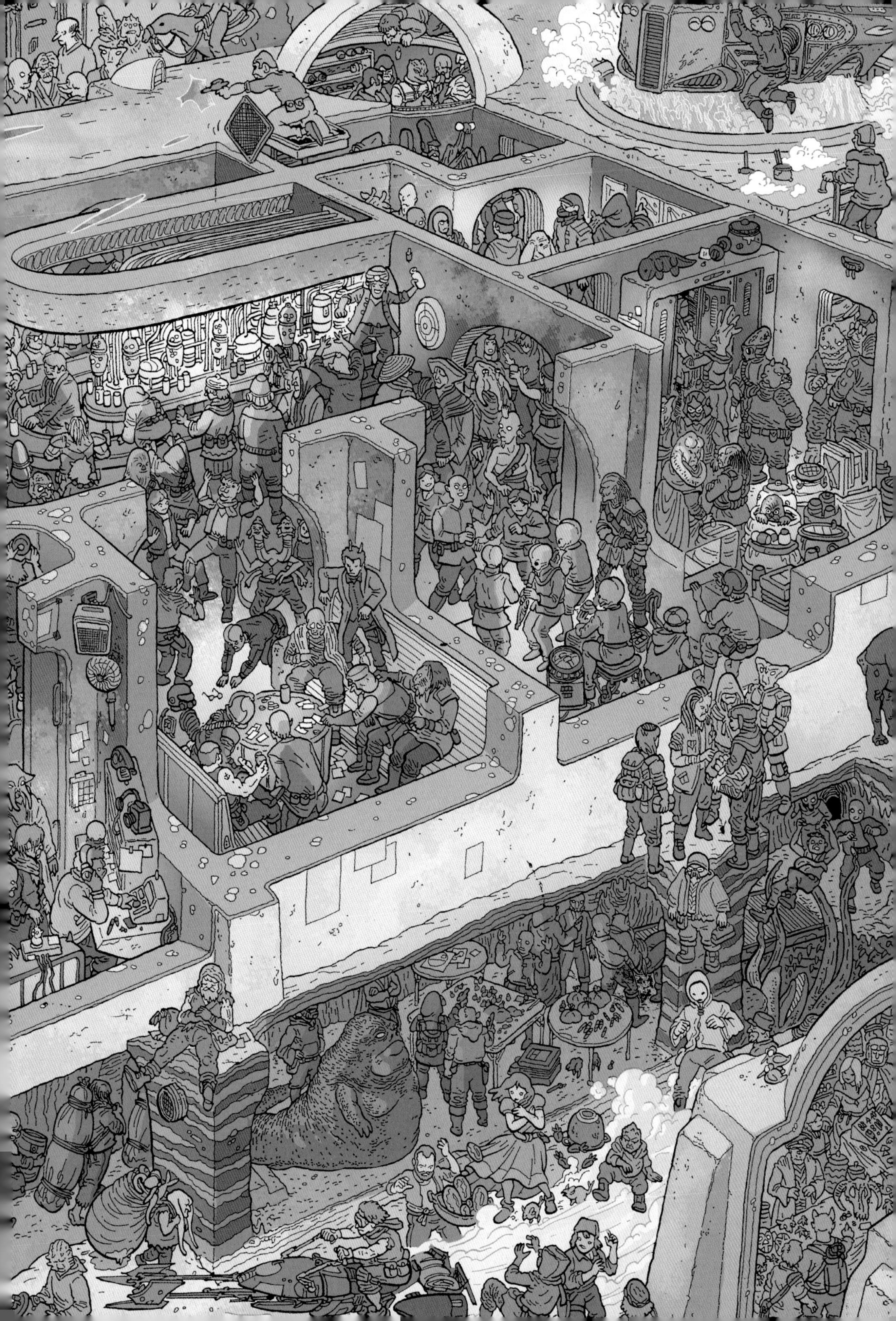

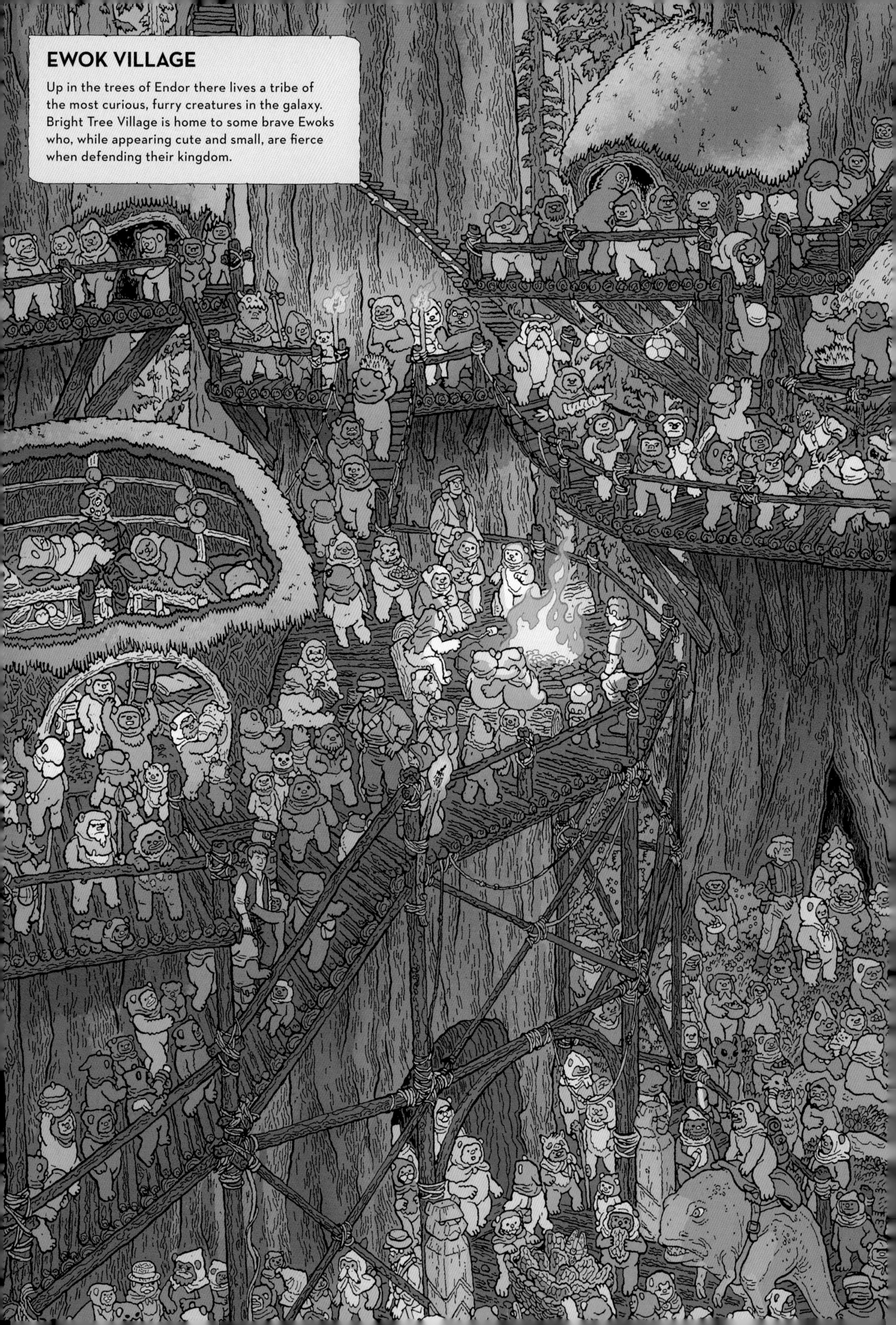
EWOK VILLAGE
Up in the trees of Endor there lives a tribe of the most curious, furry creatures in the galaxy. Bright Tree Village is home to some brave Ewoks who, while appearing cute and small, are fierce when defending their kingdom.

JEDI TEMPLE
Home to the Jedi Order, Younglings are trained here in the ways of the Force. A bit of lightsaber training, a chat with the Jedi Council, or a browse through the Jedi Archives are popular pastimes. Friends are welcome, unless you're a Sith.

THE DEATH STAR

Aboard the most powerful weapon in the universe, droids are hard at work, stormtroopers are preparing for battle, and operations to attack a rebel base are in full swing. Little do the Imperial forces know that the most notorious rebels are already in their midst.

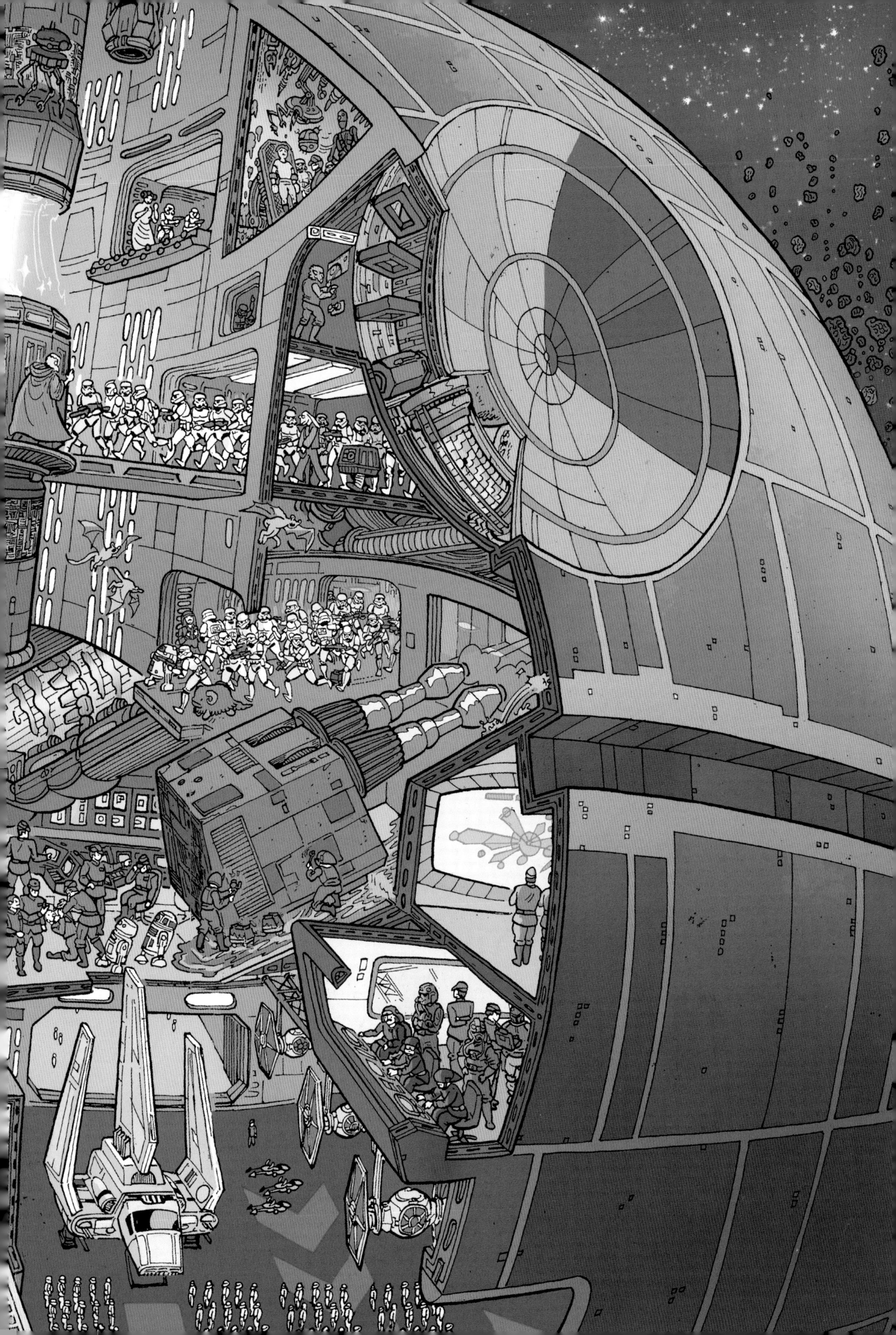

JABBA'S PALACE
In the Dune Sea on Tatooine there lives a notorious crime lord named Jabba the Hutt. Jabba controls most of Tatooine's illegal operations, and his palace is often occupied by underworld characters. Bounty hunters find fortune here collecting debts for Jabba.

IMPERIAL HANGAR
An enormous space station like the Death Star holds many Imperial ships and soldiers. When the Emperor and his henchmen arrive, the hangar must be in perfect order, with not a stormtrooper out of place, nor a rebel to be seen.

KASHYYYK

Homeworld to the mighty Wookiee race, Kashyyyk is a dangerous place for enemies. These powerful, loyal, and hairy creatures are ready for a fight, especially if protecting one of their own.

GALACTIC CHECKLIST

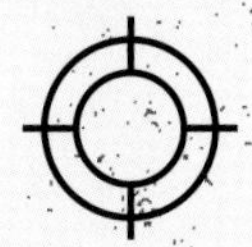

These might be a bit harder to find...

JAWA MARKET

- [ ] A Jawa feeding the birds
- [ ] Stormtrooper looking for R2-D2
- [ ] Falling Jawa
- [ ] Helmet shopper
- [ ] R5-D4
- [ ] A PIT droid
- [ ] Herd of nuna "swamp turkeys"
- [ ] An astromech strapped to a bantha
- [ ] A droid with a pincer hand
- [ ] One-eyed Jawa
- [ ] An acklay

HOTH

- [ ] A fearless Jedi
- [ ] A rebel on an Imperial speeder bike
- [ ] A rebel headfirst in the snow
- [ ] A snowball fight
- [ ] A wampa
- [ ] Rebel on a tauntaun
- [ ] 3 bungee-jumping Imperials
- [ ] Three X-wing pilots
- [ ] Rebel and snowtrooper in hand-to-hand combat
- [ ] Rebel wielding two blaster pistols
- [ ] Blue Mon Calamari

GEONOSIS

- [ ] Fighting Huttlet
- [ ] Wampa
- [ ] Droid with a warhammer
- [ ] Weapons bin
- [ ] Gungan warrior posse
- [ ] A guarlara (Naboo horse)
- [ ] Viking astromech
- [ ] One-eyed Wookiee
- [ ] Two wrestlers
- [ ] Two tough Jawas
- [ ] Two baby Geonosians
- [ ] An Ewok spectator
- [ ] An Amani archer
- [ ] 2 nexu
- [ ] 2 anoobas

CORUSCANT

- ☐ Someone enjoying the scene through viewpoint binoculars
- ☐ A Star Destroyer
- ☐ Newspaper boy
- ☐ Tourist with a dog
- ☐ A Jedi falling
- ☐ A Jawa
- ☐ The Death Star
- ☐ A Gran

MOS EISLEY

- ☐ A graffiti artist
- ☐ Baby dianoga
- ☐ Luke's landspeeder
- ☐ Garindan the Imperial spy
- ☐ Watto
- ☐ Clumsy Ortolan knocking a woman off the balcony
- ☐ Jawa pickpocketing
- ☐ Jawas stealing cable
- ☐ Jabba the Hutt receiving a new pet rancor
- ☐ Dug nomad trader

STAR DESTROYER

- ☐ An unwanted games console controller
- ☐ A discarded chicken
- ☐ Two Ewoks
- ☐ Troopers in a fist fight
- ☐ AT-ST hologram
- ☐ 1 scout trooper
- ☐ The Emperor
- ☐ Mynocks
- ☐ A mouse droid
- ☐ A black astromech
- ☐ Imperial officer dropping a folder of important papers
- ☐ Imperial officer fixing a holo-projector
- ☐ A Bothan officer
- ☐ Darth Vader's helmet
- ☐ 2 Ugnaughts

CLOUD CITY

- ☐ Man who dropped his briefcase
- ☐ Air traffic controller
- ☐ 3 yellow birds
- ☐ Mechanic who has dropped his tools
- ☐ A happy dog
- ☐ A Jawa
- ☐ An alien with a bunch of flowers
- ☐ Lando Calrissian
- ☐ Darth Vader
- ☐ Wookiee in sunglasses
- ☐ Garindan the Imperial spy

ECHO BASE

- [ ] Yoda wearing a woolly coat
- [ ] Hot drink cart
- [ ] Doughnuts
- [ ] Foam peanuts
- [ ] A speeder being polished
- [ ] Unhappy Ewoks
- [ ] A Mon Calamari
- [ ] Shield Generator
- [ ] Rebel with a fire extinguisher
- [ ] R2-D2
- [ ] Two Gonk droids
- [ ] R5 unit

THE CANTINA

- [ ] Baby Hutt
- [ ] Man trapped by sarlacc
- [ ] Clumsy speederbike rider
- [ ] Graffiti artist
- [ ] Gungan dancer
- [ ] Figrin D'an playing a happy tune
- [ ] A clock
- [ ] A dartboard
- [ ] A stormtrooper helmet
- [ ] Super battle droid
- [ ] A dice game
- [ ] A card game
- [ ] An angry chess player
- [ ] A Bith who has lost his glasses

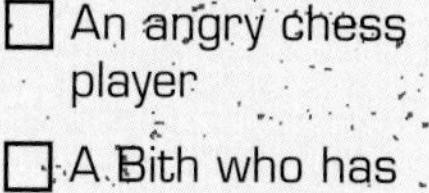

EWOK VILLAGE

- [ ] Ewok on a swing
- [ ] Ewok couple enjoying the fire
- [ ] A person drying off after an unwanted dip
- [ ] Ewok family sunbathing
- [ ] Ewok king
- [ ] Ewok carrying a pot on its head
- [ ] A sleepy lizard
- [ ] A photo opportunity
- [ ] Ewok with a winged headband
- [ ] Ewok in a bowler hat
- [ ] A leaping fish
- [ ] Ewok wearing a straw hat
- [ ] A geejaw bird resting on a stump

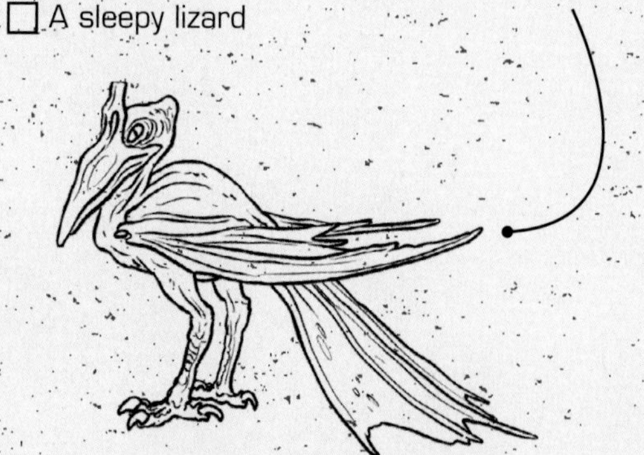

JEDI TEMPLE

- [ ] Younglings learning the Force
- [ ] Yoda
- [ ] A Padawan assembling her lightsaber
- [ ] A two-headed Jedi
- [ ] A statue with a mustache
- [ ] A bandage-wrapped alien
- [ ] A Jawa
- [ ] Sith Lord battling a Jedi
- [ ] Three Jedi Ewoks
- [ ] Boushh the bounty hunter

THE DEATH STAR

- [ ] 3 Royal Guards
- [ ] Ewoks making their escape
- [ ] A Gungan under arrest
- [ ] Imperials enjoying a movie
- [ ] A frustrated thirsty TIE fighter pilot
- [ ] Two soggy mouse droids
- [ ] A cat poster
- [ ] A snoozing stormtrooper
- [ ] Obi-Wan Kenobi
- [ ] Princess Leia
- [ ] C-3PO
- [ ] R2-D2
- [ ] Mother and child space slugs

JABBA'S PALACE

- [ ] Hidden treasure stash
- [ ] Dianoga in a toilet
- [ ] Baby opee-sea killer (fishcrab from Naboo)
- [ ] Jawa with a pet scurrier
- [ ] Young Anakin Skywalker ready for a podrace
- [ ] Monk of the B'omarr Order

IMPERIAL HANGAR

- [ ] An important visitor
- [ ] Droid mechanic
- [ ] A janitor
- [ ] An Imperial taking a photo
- [ ] Mouse droid
- [ ] A Mon Calamari officer
- [ ] Snowtrooper being inspected
- [ ] A duck-headed trooper
- [ ] Stormtrooper being inspected
- [ ] Power droid

KASHYYYK

- [ ] Yoda in a fight
- [ ] Jedi Wookiee
- [ ] General Grievous
- [ ] Wookiee wearing a Fedora
- [ ] Geonosian
- [ ] Wookiee wearing a hooded cloak
- [ ] An Ewok
- [ ] Wookiee with Leia's hairstyle
- [ ] Squad of Trandoshans

TARFFUL

BLACK KRRSANTAN

WULLFFWARRO

CHEWBACCA

GUNGI

FIND THIS WOOKIEE!

Chewbacca is hiding in every location. But watch out! Decoy Wookiees are also out and about. See how many of these hairy giants are in each location.

RORJOW

CHALKAZZA

LOHGARRA

ULIBACCA

LOCATIONS

Raarrwwr ararrrrr

Chewbacca has been spotted across the galaxy, joined by wookiee friends and rebel allies for you to find. But beware! The following locations also have enemies from the Empire and First Order.

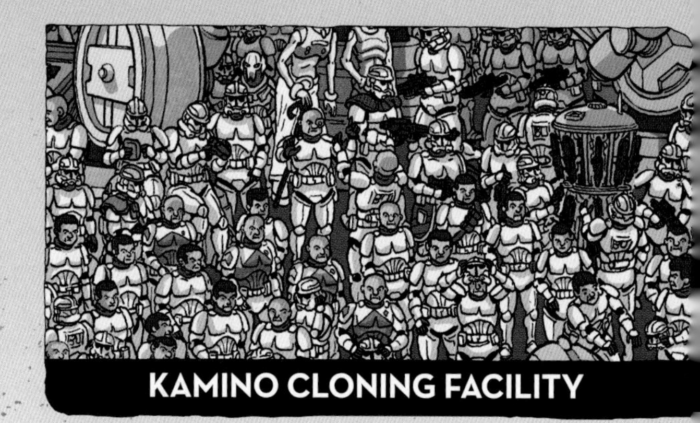

KAMINO CLONING FACILITY

DROID FACTORY

OTOH GUNGA

LOTHAL

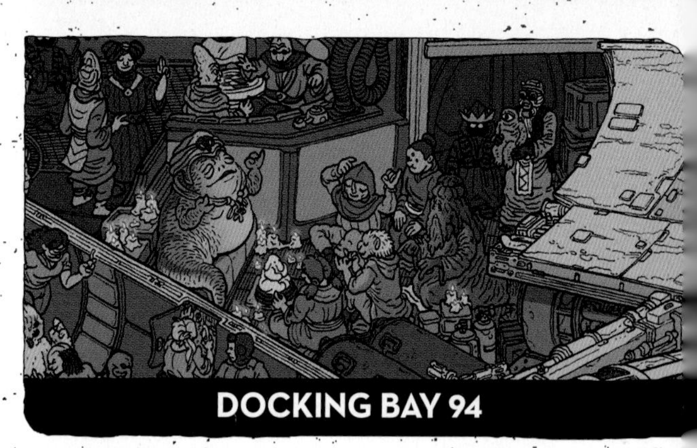

DOCKING BAY 94

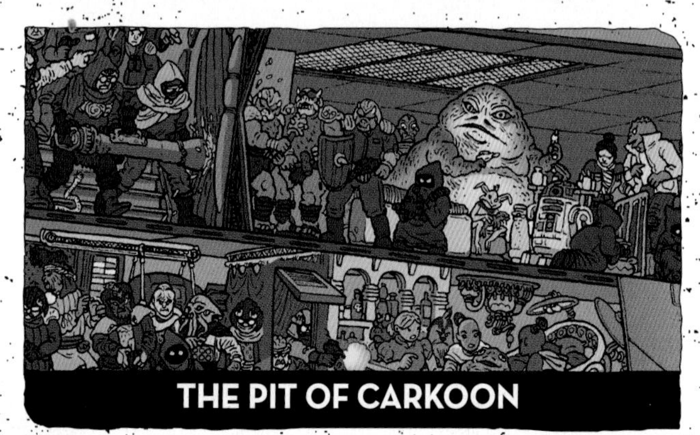

THE PIT OF CARKOON

HOME ONE

JEDHA

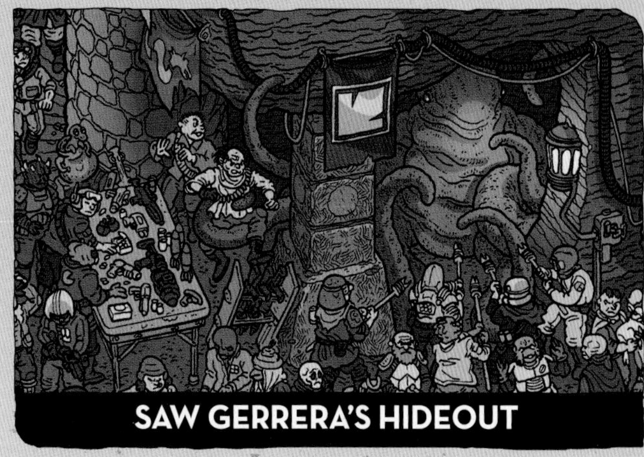

SAW GERRERA'S HIDEOUT

SCARIF

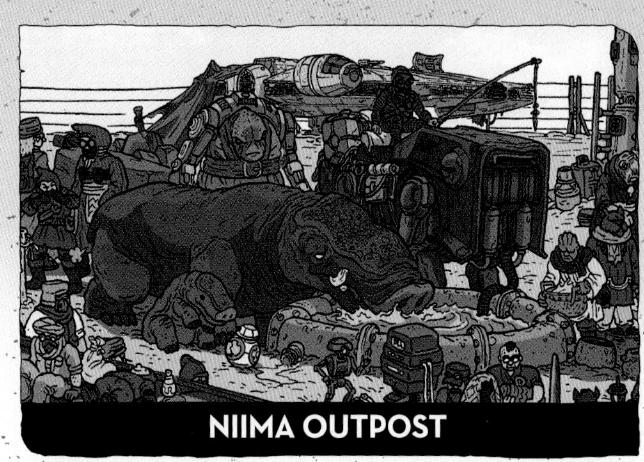

NIIMA OUTPOST

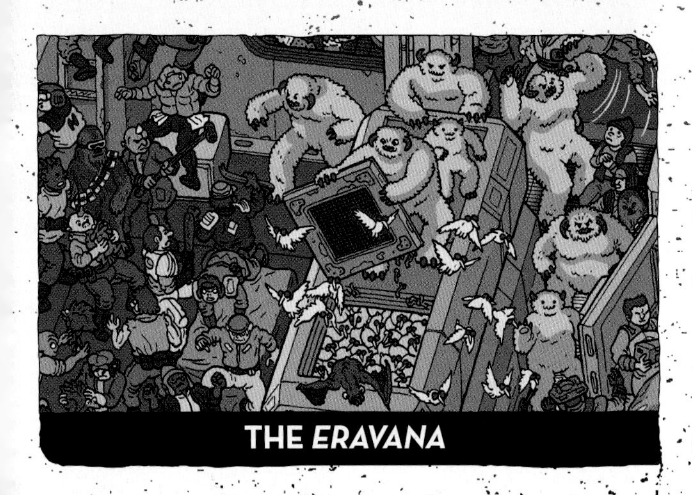

THE *ERAVANA*

MAZ KANATA'S CASTLE

STARKILLER BASE

RESISTANCE BASE

KAMINO CLONING FACILITY

On an aquatic planet south of the Rishi Maze lives a tall, elegant race called the Kaminoans. They are well known for their cloning technology and are tasked with building an army vitally important to the Galactic Republic.

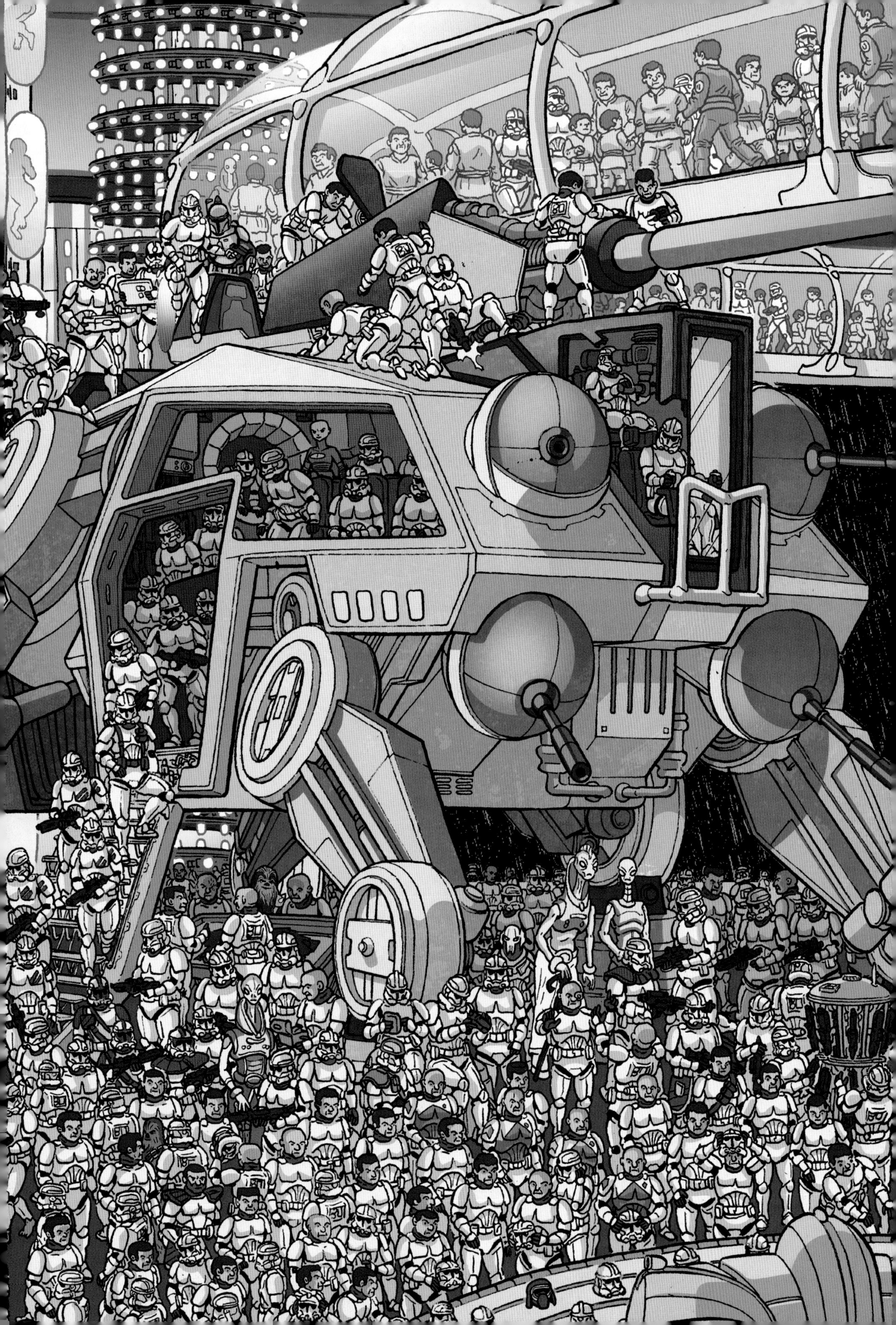

DROID FACTORY
The Geonosians are a technologically advanced species, making their homeworld an ideal place for a massive battle droid foundry. Each facility houses hundreds of conveyor belts capable of creating thousands of droids a day.
COUNT DOOKU
POGGLE THE LESSER
R2-D2
C-3PO
WAT TAMBOR
SHU MAI

OTOH GUNGA
Beneath the waters of Naboo lies a city of bubbles: a series of buildings created by the amphibious Gungans. They are a proud warrior race that, despite their peaceful nature, would do anything to protect their home.
JAR JAR BINKS
PADMÉ AMIDALA
RISH LOO
AHSOKA
ANAKIN SKYWALKER
BOSS NASS

LOTHAL
A planet in the Outer Rim territories, Lothal was in such economic hardship that its people invited the Empire with open arms. Now disillusioned with their oppressors, some Lothalites welcome the appearance of rebel cells, black-market activity, and all-out resistance to the Imperial regime.
HERA
EZRA
KANAN
SABINE
INQUISITOR
CHOPPER

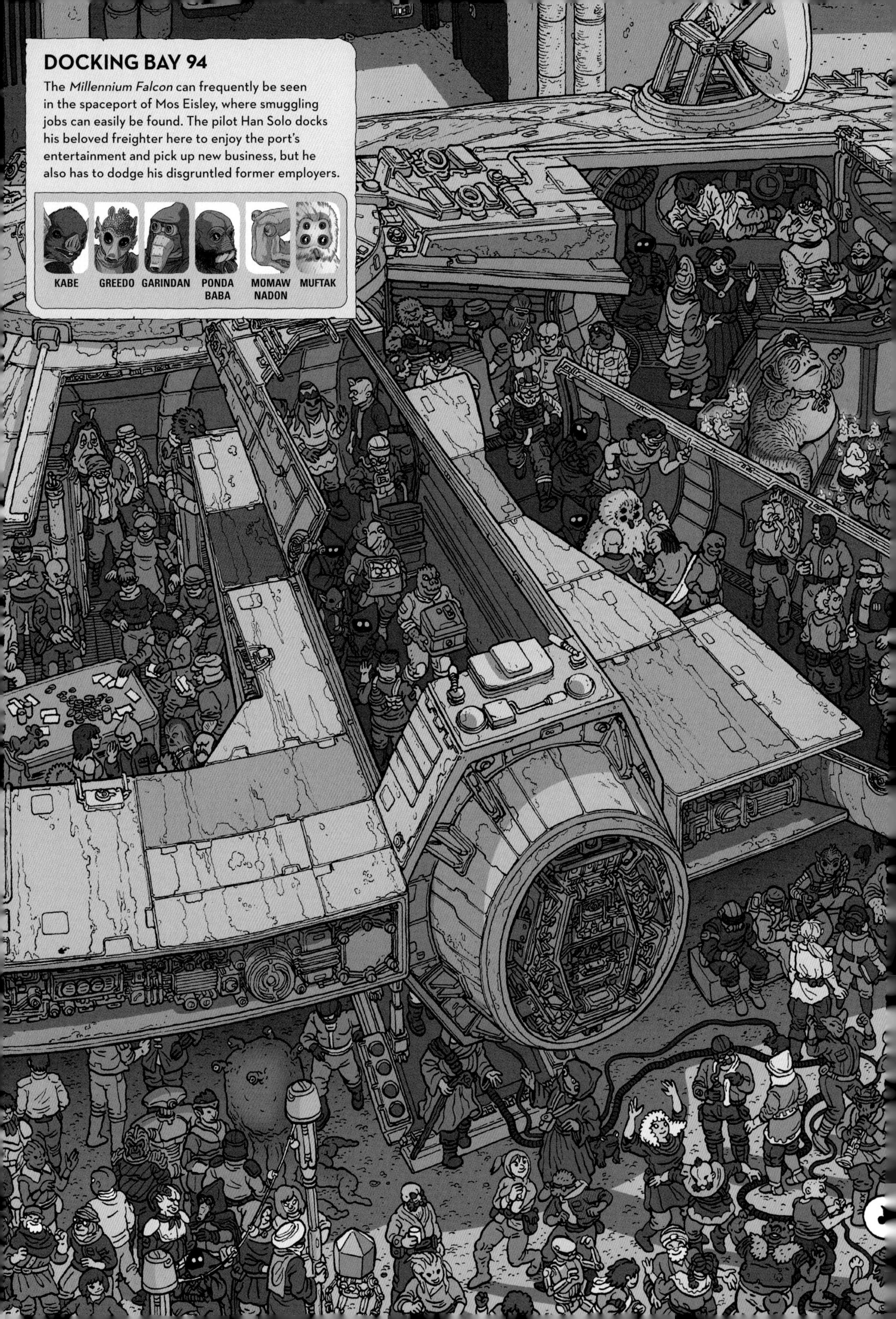
DOCKING BAY 94
The *Millennium Falcon* can frequently be seen in the spaceport of Mos Eisley, where smuggling jobs can easily be found. The pilot Han Solo docks his beloved freighter here to enjoy the port's entertainment and pick up new business, but he also has to dodge his disgruntled former employers.
KABE
GREEDO
GARINDAN
PONDA BABA
MOMAW NADON
MUFTAK

THE PIT OF CARKOON
In the desert of Tatooine lies a giant pit, which is home to a terrifying creature known as the sarlacc. Crime lord Jabba the Hutt uses the pit to frighten his enemies and frequently visits it aboard his sail barge, the Khetanna.
HAN SOLO
BOBA FETT
BIB FORTUNA
BOUSHH
MAX REBO
EV-9D9

HOME ONE
Home One was originally built to explore deep space, but now serves as a military vessel and is armed with ion cannons, turbolasers, and several tractor beams. This star cruiser is the largest and most advanced ship in the Alliance Fleet, making it a crucial base of operations for the rebel cause.
PRINCESS LEIA
GENERAL MADINE
WEDGE ANTILLES
2-1B
LANDO CALRISSIAN
NIEN NUNB

JEDHA
This ancient desert moon is rich in kyber crystals and therefore of great significance to the Empire. Though occupied by Imperial forces, the deeply spiritual people of Jedha continue to worship the Force and welcome pilgrims to the Holy City.
SILVANIE PHEST
KULLBEE SPERADO
WEETEEF
K-2SO
BEEZER FORTUNA
MOROFF

SAW GERRERA'S HIDEOUT
Coordinating a rebellion against the occupying forces on Jedha, Saw Gerrera is a familiar face in the fight against the Empire. Now bunkered down in his secluded caves, Saw has his gang of rebels carry out brutal missions to destabilize the regime.
G2-1B7
CYCYED OCK
LEEVAN TENZA
MAGVA YARRO
EDRIO
SAW GERRERA

SCARIF
This remote tropical planet is home to an Imperial military base with a terrifying secret. The facility is being used to construct a planet-destroying superweapon, the Death Star. Scarif is protected by a deflector shield, but it can be entered through a shield gate.
JYN
CASSIAN
BAZE
CHIRRUT
BODHI
KRENNIC

NIIMA OUTPOST

Jakku is an ideal place for scavengers due to its many great shipwrecks from a long-ago battle between the Empire and Rebellion. The ruthless Unkar Plutt has a stronghold on the settlement where these scavengers come to trade their finds.

THE *ERAVANA*
After losing the *Millennium Falcon*, Han and Chewie came into possession of a large heavy freighter and used it to resume their smuggling career. The *Eravana* is not well-armed, nor is it as fast as the *Falcon*, but it does have the space for a lot of strange cargo, including frightening livestock.
FINN
HAN SOLO
TASU LEECH
REY
BALA-TIK
BB-8

MAZ KANATA'S CASTLE
On the planet Takodana lives a pirate queen, who allows smugglers to reside in her ancient castle. Maz has strict rules against violence, so travelers from across the galaxy can find refuge here from bounty hunters and political enemies.
MAZ KANATA
HAN SOLO
CRIMSON CORSAIR
GRUMMGAR
BAZINE NETAL
EMMIE

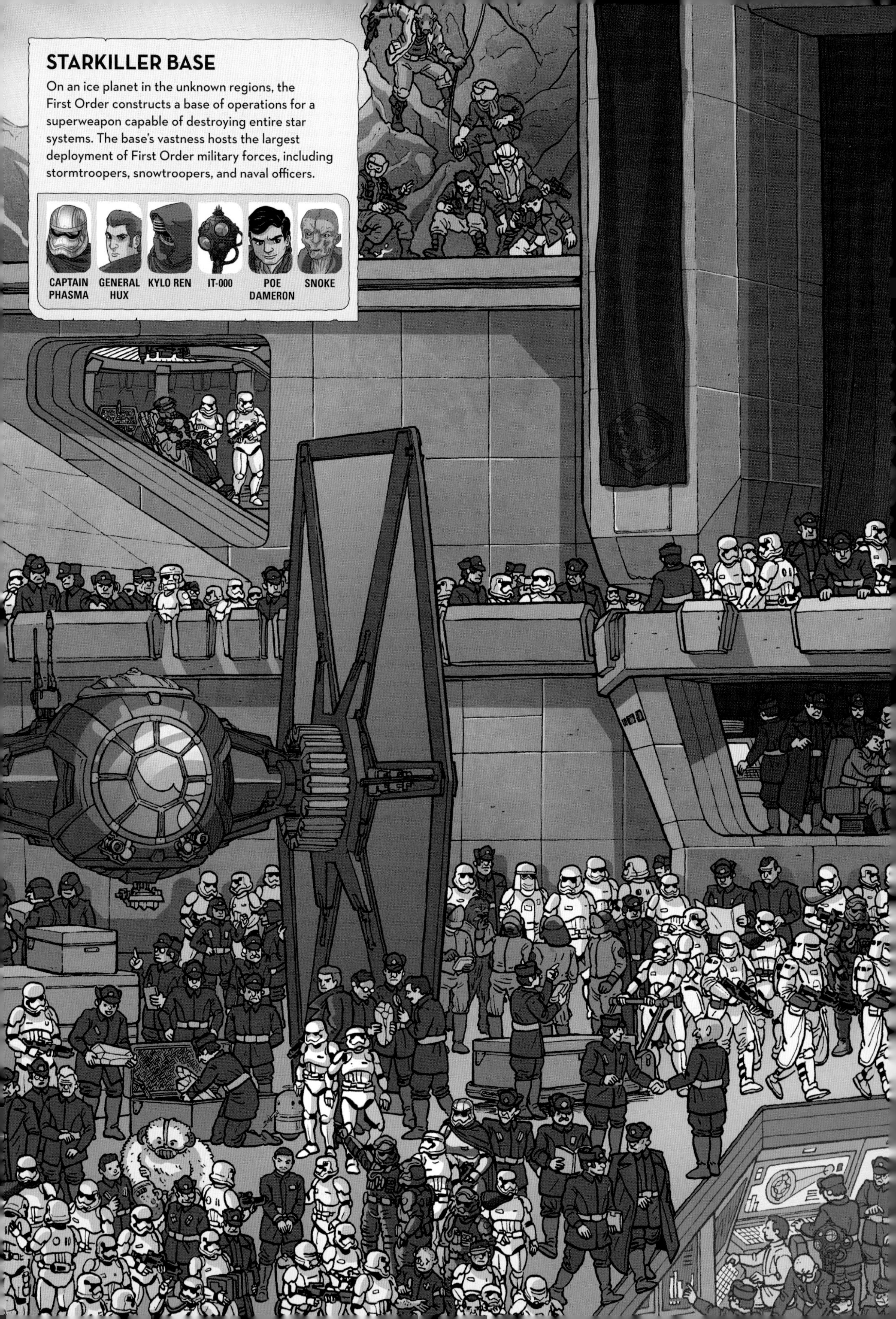
STARKILLER BASE
On an ice planet in the unknown regions, the First Order constructs a base of operations for a superweapon capable of destroying entire star systems. The base's vastness hosts the largest deployment of First Order military forces, including stormtroopers, snowtroopers, and naval officers.
CAPTAIN PHASMA
GENERAL HUX
KYLO REN
IT-000
POE DAMERON
SNOKE

RESISTANCE BASE
The Resistance headquarters is surrounded by thick jungle and the command center is underground, meaning the facility is well concealed from enemy sensors. Multiple hangars hold the Resistance Fleet including the all-important X-wings.
POE DAMERON
ELLO ASTY
GENERAL LEIA
FINN
NIEN NUNB
PZ-4CO

GALACTIC CHECKLIST

These might be a bit harder to find...

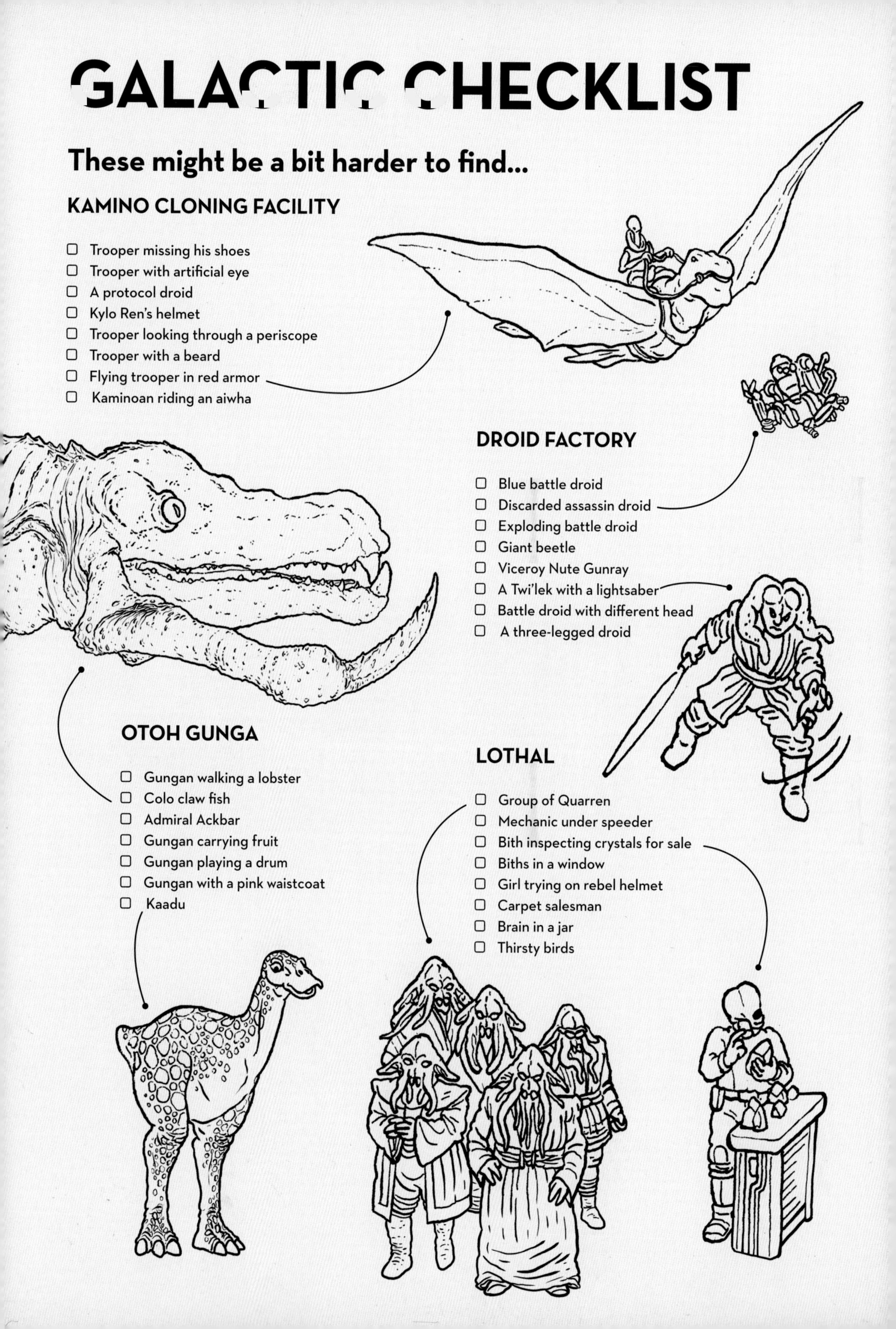

KAMINO CLONING FACILITY

- ☐ Trooper missing his shoes
- ☐ Trooper with artificial eye
- ☐ A protocol droid
- ☐ Kylo Ren's helmet
- ☐ Trooper looking through a periscope
- ☐ Trooper with a beard
- ☐ Flying trooper in red armor
- ☐ Kaminoan riding an aiwha

DROID FACTORY

- ☐ Blue battle droid
- ☐ Discarded assassin droid
- ☐ Exploding battle droid
- ☐ Giant beetle
- ☐ Viceroy Nute Gunray
- ☐ A Twi'lek with a lightsaber
- ☐ Battle droid with different head
- ☐ A three-legged droid

OTOH GUNGA

- ☐ Gungan walking a lobster
- ☐ Colo claw fish
- ☐ Admiral Ackbar
- ☐ Gungan carrying fruit
- ☐ Gungan playing a drum
- ☐ Gungan with a pink waistcoat
- ☐ Kaadu

LOTHAL

- ☐ Group of Quarren
- ☐ Mechanic under speeder
- ☐ Bith inspecting crystals for sale
- ☐ Biths in a window
- ☐ Girl trying on rebel helmet
- ☐ Carpet salesman
- ☐ Brain in a jar
- ☐ Thirsty birds

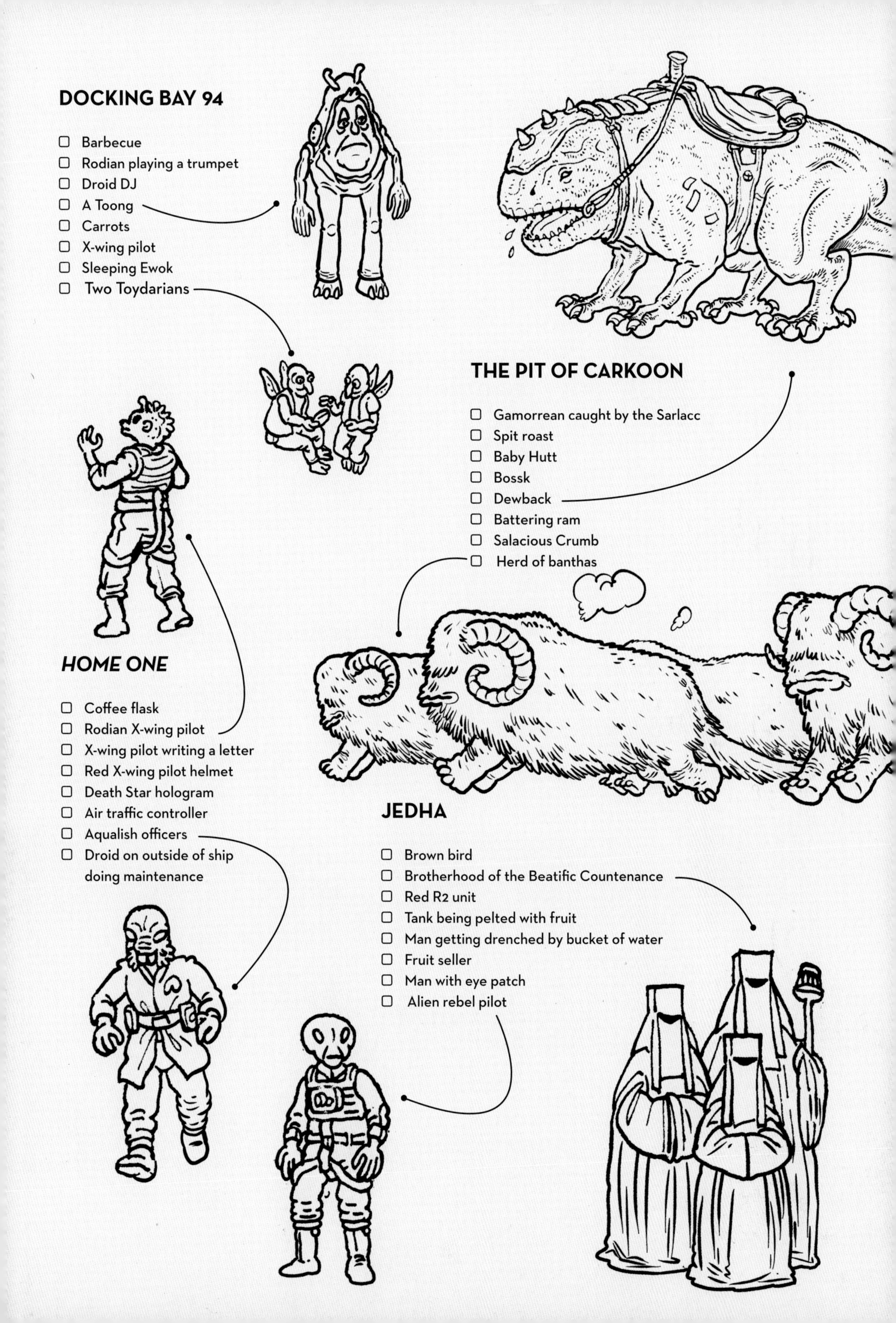

DOCKING BAY 94

- ☐ Barbecue
- ☐ Rodian playing a trumpet
- ☐ Droid DJ
- ☐ A Toong
- ☐ Carrots
- ☐ X-wing pilot
- ☐ Sleeping Ewok
- ☐ Two Toydarians

THE PIT OF CARKOON

- ☐ Gamorrean caught by the Sarlacc
- ☐ Spit roast
- ☐ Baby Hutt
- ☐ Bossk
- ☐ Dewback
- ☐ Battering ram
- ☐ Salacious Crumb
- ☐ Herd of banthas

HOME ONE

- ☐ Coffee flask
- ☐ Rodian X-wing pilot
- ☐ X-wing pilot writing a letter
- ☐ Red X-wing pilot helmet
- ☐ Death Star hologram
- ☐ Air traffic controller
- ☐ Aqualish officers
- ☐ Droid on outside of ship doing maintenance

JEDHA

- ☐ Brown bird
- ☐ Brotherhood of the Beatific Countenance
- ☐ Red R2 unit
- ☐ Tank being pelted with fruit
- ☐ Man getting drenched by bucket of water
- ☐ Fruit seller
- ☐ Man with eye patch
- ☐ Alien rebel pilot

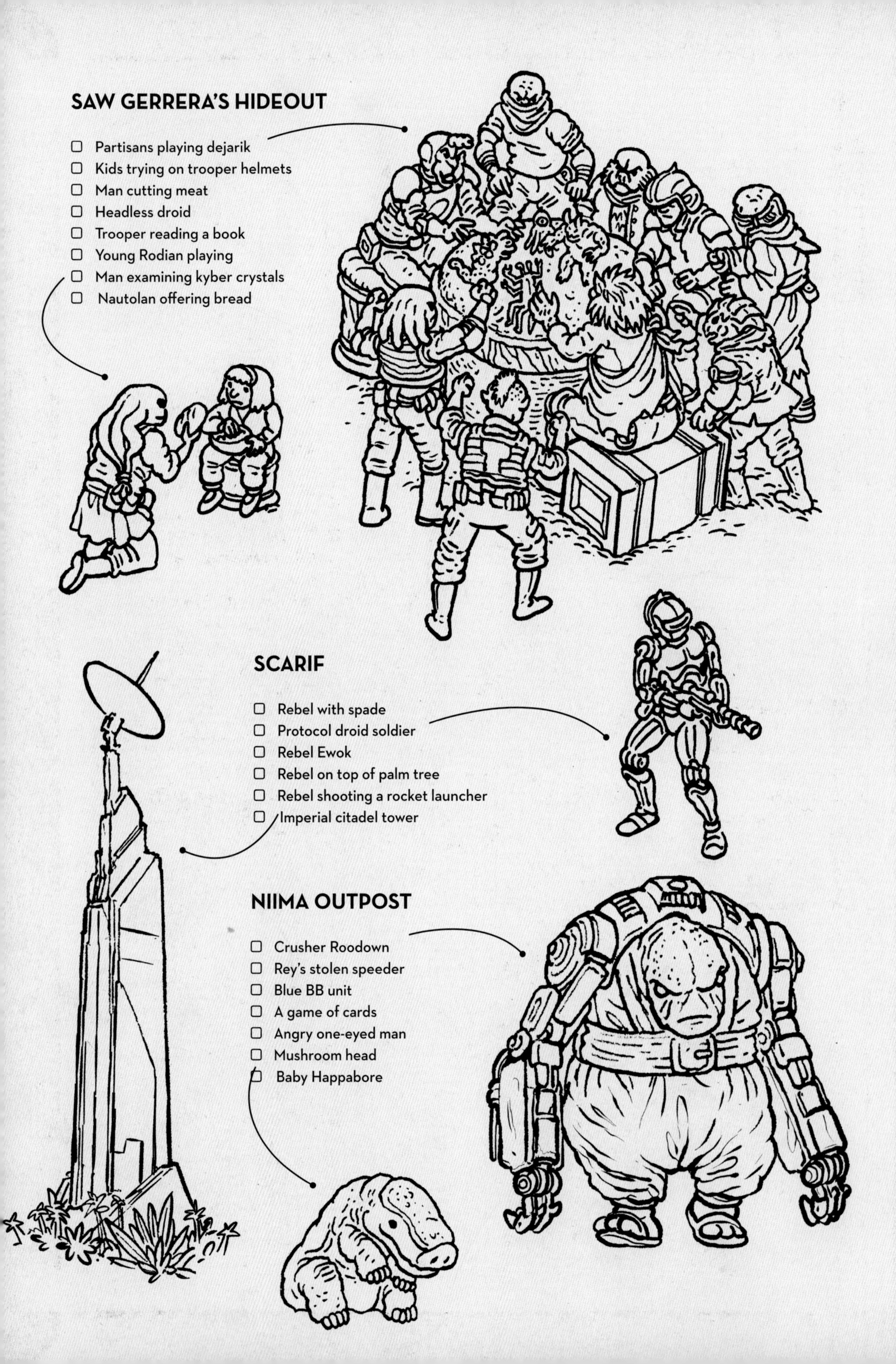

SAW GERRERA'S HIDEOUT

- ☐ Partisans playing dejarik
- ☐ Kids trying on trooper helmets
- ☐ Man cutting meat
- ☐ Headless droid
- ☐ Trooper reading a book
- ☐ Young Rodian playing
- ☐ Man examining kyber crystals
- ☐ Nautolan offering bread

SCARIF

- ☐ Rebel with spade
- ☐ Protocol droid soldier
- ☐ Rebel Ewok
- ☐ Rebel on top of palm tree
- ☐ Rebel shooting a rocket launcher
- ☐ Imperial citadel tower

NIIMA OUTPOST

- ☐ Crusher Roodown
- ☐ Rey's stolen speeder
- ☐ Blue BB unit
- ☐ A game of cards
- ☐ Angry one-eyed man
- ☐ Mushroom head
- ☐ Baby Happabore